Peppa Pig

and the
Treasure Hunt

This book is based on the TV series *Peppa Pig*.
Peppa Pig is created by Neville Astley and Mark Baker.
Peppa Pig © Astley Baker Davies Ltd/Entertainment One U.K. Limited 2003.
www.peppapig.com

First edition 2015

Library of Congress Catalog Card Number 2014939354
ISBN 978-0-7636-7703-9

14 15 16 17 18 19 SCP 10 9 8 7 6 5 4 3 2 1

Printed in Humen, Dongguan, China

This book was typeset in Peppa.
The illustrations were created digitally.

Candlewick Entertainment
An imprint of Candlewick Press
99 Dover Street
Somerville, Massachusetts 02144

visit us at www.candlewick.com

Peppa Pig and the Treasure Hunt

CANDLEWICK
ENTERTAINMENT

Peppa Pig and her little brother, George, are very excited.
They are going to spend the day with Granny Pig and Grandpa Pig.

"Off we go!"
says Daddy Pig.

"Hello, Peppa. Hello, George!" says Granny Pig.
"Ahoy there, me hearties!" says Grandpa.

"We have a surprise for you!"
Granny and Grandpa Pig say.

Peppa and George love surprises.
"It's a treasure hunt!" says Granny Pig.

"Grandpa buried treasure somewhere in the yard.
It's up to you two to find it."

Treasure!

George wants to find it. Peppa wants to find it, too.

Peppa has never searched for treasure before.
"How do we find it?" she asks.

"Follow the map!" says Granny.

"Hooray!"
says Peppa.

Grandpa Pig gives George the pirate hat.

"Arrr,"
says George.

Something isn't quite right.
"I don't understand the map,"
says Peppa.
"Can you help, Daddy?"

"Oh, yes," says Daddy Pig.
"I'm very good with maps.
Hmmm,
this map *is* difficult."

"You're holding it upside down," says Granny Pig.

"**Whoops!**" says Daddy. Everyone laughs.

"I see," says Peppa. "It's easy.
X marks the spot where the treasure is buried!
It's right between two apple trees.
But where are they?"

"You have to find the clues," says Granny Pig.
"The first one is in a bottle."

Peppa and George search.
They find a scarecrow.

They find butterflies.

They find frogs.

George finds something else.

"That's not treasure," says Peppa.

"I see it!" cries Peppa.
She and George rush down
into the yard.
"It's a message in a bottle!"

Peppa hands the message
to Mummy Pig to read.
"This pirate has very bad handwriting,"
says Mummy Pig.
"I can't make it out at all."

"Nonsense," says Grandpa Pig.

"It says to find the arrows and follow them."

Peppa and George follow the arrows
to the tree house,

past the
chicken coop,

and behind the beehive.

They follow them up, down,
and all around the yard.

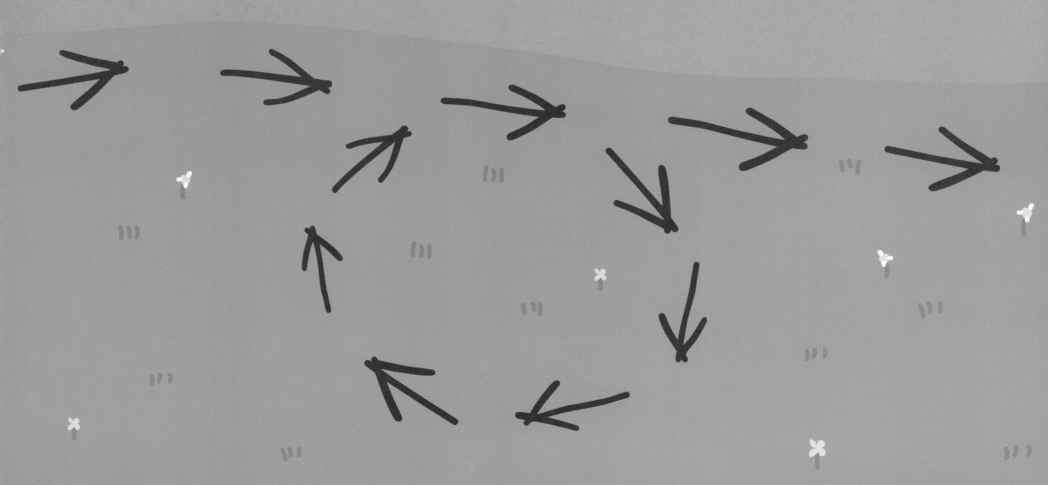

At the last arrow, Peppa sees something bright and shiny on the ground. "A key!"

"I wonder what it will unlock," says Peppa.

Peppa looks up. She points.
"An apple tree!" she says.

George points, and Peppa says,
"Another apple tree!"

Daddy gets a shovel.
He digs and digs
and digs.
Finally the shovel hits
something hard.

"What is it?" asks Peppa. Daddy reaches down into the hole. . . .

"A treasure chest!"

cries Peppa.

"Oooh,"

says George.

Peppa uses the key to unlock the chest. It is filled with shiny coins.
"Gold coins," says Peppa. "We're rich!"
"Oooh," says George.

"These are better than gold coins," says Grandpa Pig.
"These coins are made of chocolate."

"OOOOH!" say Peppa and George.

"**Mmmm,**" says Peppa.

"This is the best treasure ever!"